DAISYLOCKS

by Marianne Berkes
illustrated by Cathy Morrison

Daisylocks wasn't happy where she had been planted. Maybe there was a better place where Daisylocks could live and thrive, so she asked the wind to help her.

"I can do that," said Wind. He picked her up and blew her to a hot, dry desert.

But Daisylocks didn't like it there. "I can't get enough water here. I'm burning up. This place is much too hot!"

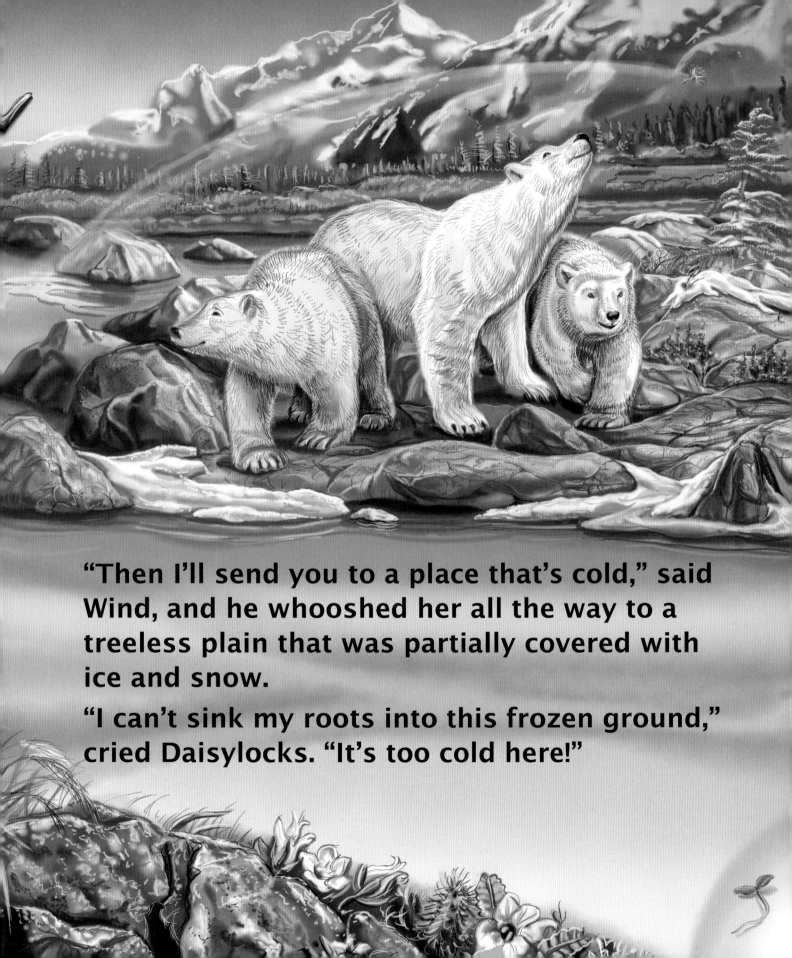

"Then I'll send you to a place that's cold," said Wind, and he whooshed her all the way to a treeless plain that was partially covered with ice and snow.

"I can't sink my roots into this frozen ground," cried Daisylocks. "It's too cold here!"

"Maybe you should go back home," wailed Wind, "where it is *just right*!"

"I'm not ready to do that yet," said Daisylocks. "There's got to be a better place to put my roots down."

"Well," suggested Wind, "why don't I just blow you around until you see a place you like?" And Wind did just that.

Daisylocks looked down at different landscapes as Wind kept her in the air.

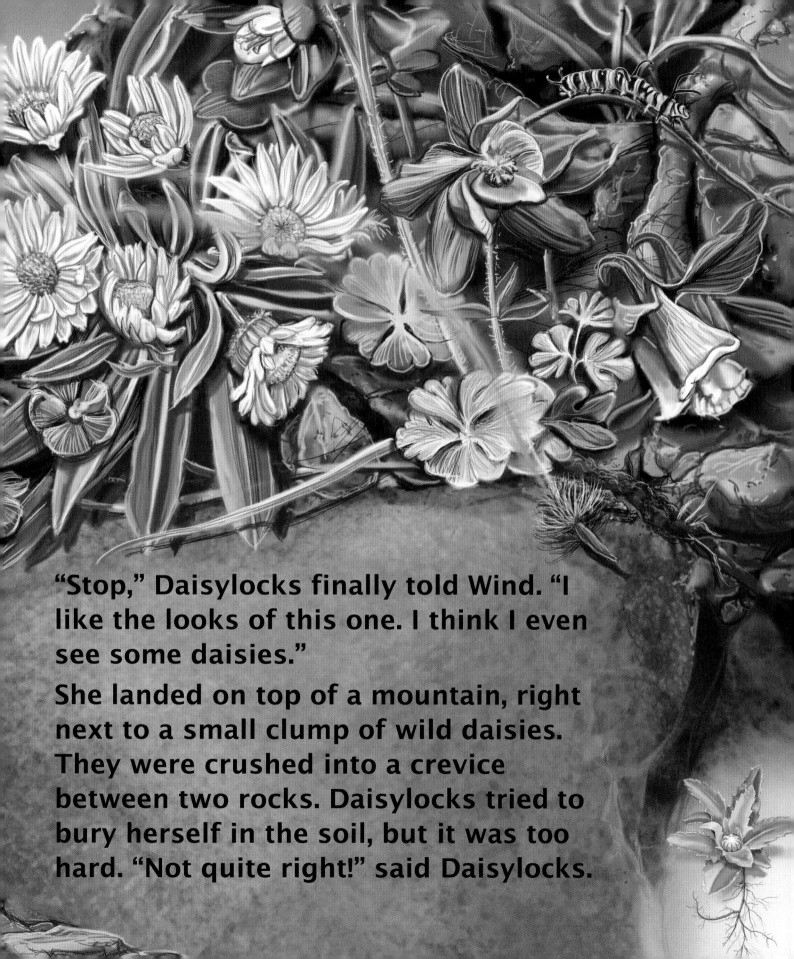

"Stop," Daisylocks finally told Wind. "I like the looks of this one. I think I even see some daisies."

She landed on top of a mountain, right next to a small clump of wild daisies. They were crushed into a crevice between two rocks. Daisylocks tried to bury herself in the soil, but it was too hard. "Not quite right!" said Daisylocks.

Wind came back, picked her up, and whisked her away to a wetland area in the Everglades.

"No," said Daisylocks, "this is definitely not right for me. It's too soft and wet."

"But I see some pretty daisies," said Wind.

"Well, they are actually more like weeds. I, on the other hand, need to be cultivated by hand."

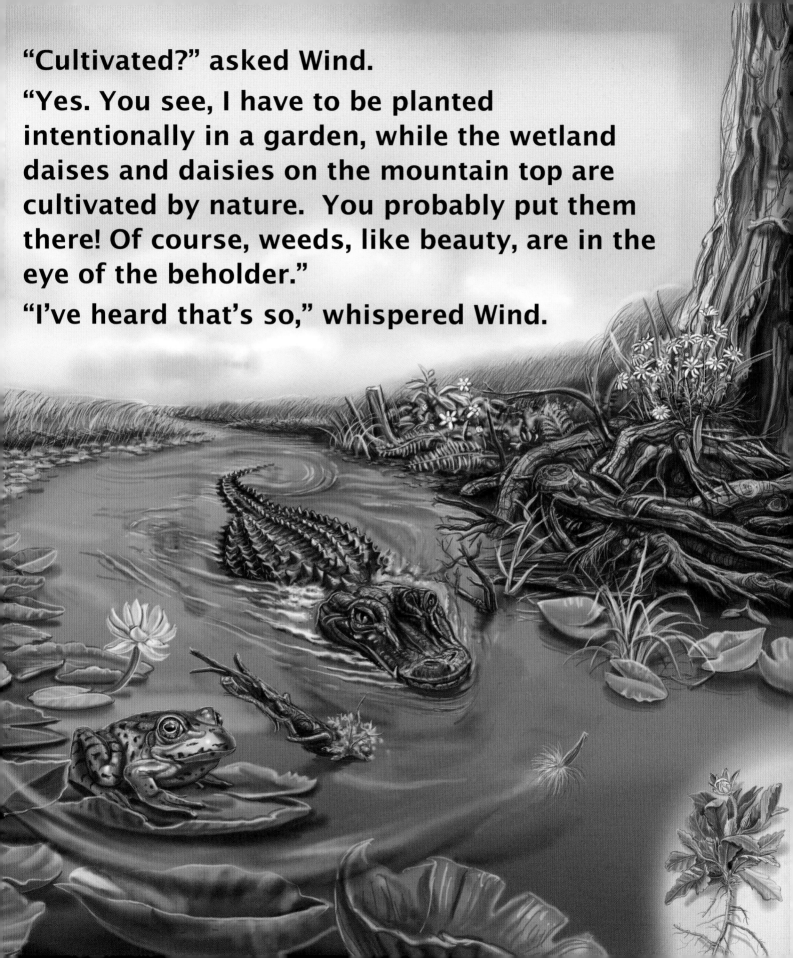

"Cultivated?" asked Wind.

"Yes. You see, I have to be planted intentionally in a garden, while the wetland daises and daisies on the mountain top are cultivated by nature. You probably put them there! Of course, weeds, like beauty, are in the eye of the beholder."

"I've heard that's so," whispered Wind.

"I'm really getting hungry," said Daisylocks. "I need to anchor my roots, so I can be fed and start growing."

"Let me think," said Wind.

"I'm not giving up! Once my roots are established, I can grow as a perennial."

"A perennial?" asked Wind.

"It's a plant that grows for more than one year," answered Daisylocks. "Some plants are perennials, while others are annuals and survive for just one year!"

"Well," said Wind, "I know of a place where you could live for years and years in a warm, humid environment. That should be *just right*!"

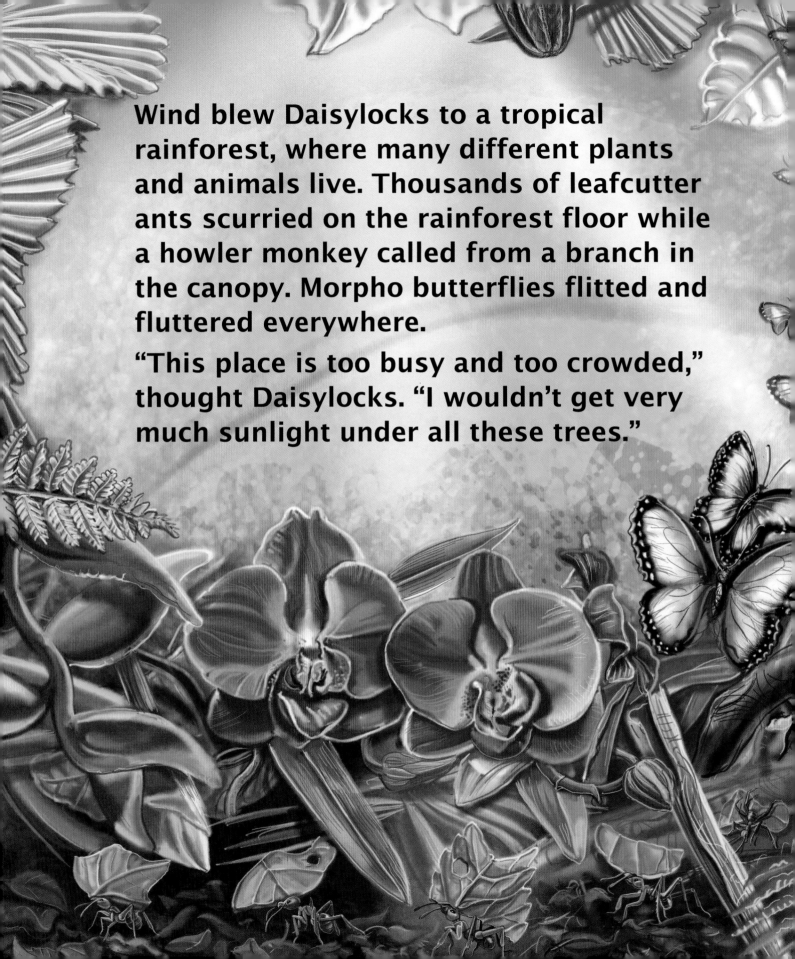

Wind blew Daisylocks to a tropical rainforest, where many different plants and animals live. Thousands of leafcutter ants scurried on the rainforest floor while a howler monkey called from a branch in the canopy. Morpho butterflies flitted and fluttered everywhere.

"This place is too busy and too crowded," thought Daisylocks. "I wouldn't get very much sunlight under all these trees."

"I need room to spread out," Daisylocks told Wind, "and I need lots of sunlight. Can't we find somewhere else?"

"I think I know," said Wind, "a place that's *just right*!"

"You said that before," Daisylocks reminded him. "So far it's been too hot, too cold, too hard, too soft, and now too crowded."

Wind whooshed Daisylocks to a faraway beach with lots of room and lots of sun.

The sand glistened in the sunlight as a seagull perched on a post near some rambling sea grape vines. Daisylocks could see miles of beach, and miles and miles of ocean. There was certainly room to spread out. Daisylocks was already enjoying the warm sun. But when she tried to put her roots down, the sand was way too loose. "My roots will never hold here," said Daisylocks.

"Let me guess," whispered Wind. "It's not *just right*?"

"I've been to places that are too hot, too cold, too hard, too soft, too crowded, and too sandy," said Daisylocks.

"You know what?" said Wind. "I'm going to whoosh you home so you can bloom where you were planted. *That* is where it is *just right!*"

For Creative Minds

Basic Needs of Plants

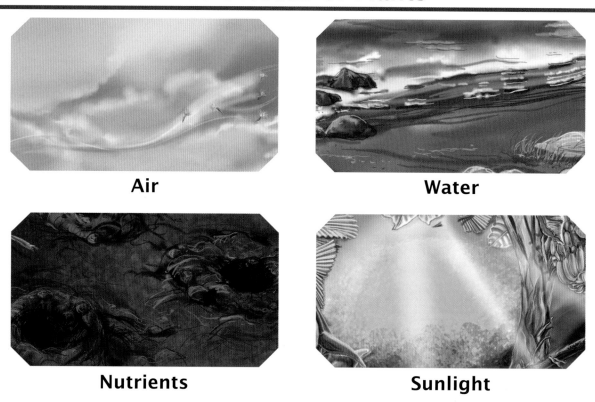

Air

Water

Nutrients

Sunlight

Plants need food to grow. Unlike animals, plants make their own food through a process called **photosynthesis**! In order to do this, they need four things: air, water, nutrients and sunlight.

Plants use their leaves to take in carbon dioxide from the air. Making food takes a lot of energy! Plants use the energy from sunlight to create their sugary food from water and carbon dioxide in the air.

Plants absorb nutrients and water from the soil. Different types of plants live in different types of soil. Soils can be fine or coarse. Some types of soils hold more water than others. Plants can live in salt water or fresh water. Some plants need a lot of water to grow, but other plants may only need a little water.

Different plants grow in different climates. Each plant needs the weather and temperature of their own climates to help them survive.

Match the Habitats

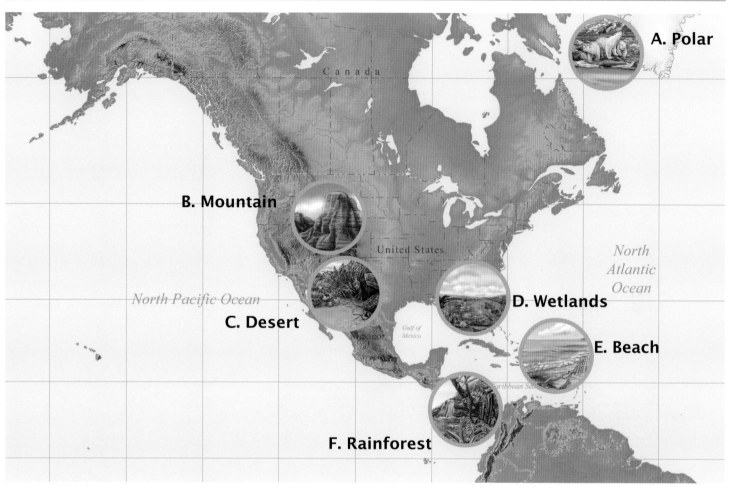

A. Polar

B. Mountain

C. Desert

D. Wetlands

E. Beach

F. Rainforest

Match the habitat to its location on the map.

1. This habitat has a cold climate.

2. Sandy soil and strong winds make this salty habitat a difficult place for plants to grow.

3. High above sea-level, the air in this habitat is thin and the surface is rocky and steep.

4. This wet habitat has little solid ground in which to plant roots.

5. Crowded trees in this habitat block most of the sunlight from plants on the ground.

6. This hot climate has very little water.

Plant Parts

Just like animals, plants have many different parts. These different parts help the plant to grow, live, and reproduce.

Like all living things, plants need to reproduce. **Flowers** hold spores that can join together to create seeds that will grow into new plants. These spores are carried by the wind or by pollinating insects and animals, like bees. Some flowers produce **fruits**. Fruits have seeds that can grow into full plants.

Plants absorb energy from sunlight through their **leaves**. Leaves are usually green and are often thin and flat, with as much surface area as possible exposed to the sun.

The **stem** (or **trunk** on larger, woody plants) supports the weight of the plant and holds the flowers and leaves up off the ground.

A plant absorbs water and nutrients through its **roots**. The roots are usually below the ground and anchor the plant in place so it doesn't fall over or blow away.

Match the Plant

A.

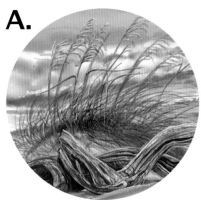

sea oats

B.

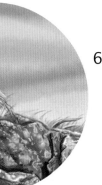

water lillies

C.

lichen

1. This **desert** plant has thick, waxy skin that helps the plant retain water. Spiny needles protect the plant against animals trying to get to the water inside.

2. Most plants on the **tundra** do not grow very tall. They stay low to the ground to avoid the icy wind. Many arctic plants have shallow roots because the frozen earth is too hard to dig into. This plant-like fungus uses its shallow roots to attach to rocks.

3. Plants in the **rainforest** live in a hot, wet habitat. This rainforest tree has thin, smooth bark and large ridges. These adaptations make it easy for air and water to enter and leave the tree.

4. This **wetland** plant doesn't need land to grow. Its roots absorb nutrients from the water. Thick, flat leaves help it float and provide shade for fish and other animals below.

5. Plants on the **beach** adapt to a salty, sandy environment with strong winds. This beach plant has long, deep roots that hold on tight to the loose soil. The tall blades of grass are flexible, so they can bend in heavy winds.

6. The rocky face of the **mountain** is a good home for this tree. The bark is thick and scaly, and the needle-like leaves stay on all year round.

D.

cactus

E.

pine tree

F.

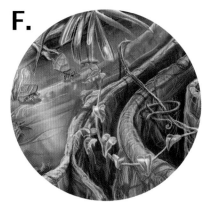

kapok tree

For the ten wonderful illustrators, including Cathy Morrison, of course, who have made the words in my picture books come alive with their amazing talents. All 17 books are "just right."—MB

In memory of Mildred Morrison. As moms go, she was "just right!"—CM

Thanks to Jaclyn Stallard, Manager of Education Programs at Project Learning Tree (www.plt.org), for verifying the accuracy of the information in this book.

Library of Congress Cataloging-in-Publication Data

Berkes, Marianne Collins, author.
 Daisylocks / by Marianne Berkes ; illustrated by Cathy Morrison.
    pages cm
   ISBN 978-1-62855-206-5 (English hardcover) -- ISBN 978-1-62855-215-7 (English pbk.) -- ISBN 978-1-62855-233-1 (Englsih ebook downloadable) -- ISBN 978-1-62855-251-5 (English ebook dual language enhanced) 1. Daisies--Habitat--Juvenile literature. 2. Winds--Juvenile literature. I. Morrison, Cathy, illustrator. II. Title.
   QK495.C74B43 2014
   583'.99--dc23
                            2013036736
Also available in Spanish:
9781628552249   Spanish paperback ISBN
9781628552423   Spanish eBook downloadable ISBN
9781628552607   Interactive, read-aloud eBook featuring selectable English and
Spanish text and audio (web and iPad/tablet based) ISBN - Spanish

Daisylocks: Original title in English
La plantita Margarita: Spanish title

Lexile® Level: 640
key phrases for educators: basic needs: plants, climate, earth
properties: soil, habitat

Manufactured in China, December 2013
This product conforms to CPSIA 2008
First Printing

Sylvan Dell Publishing
Mt. Pleasant, SC 29464
www.SylvanDellPublishing.com